Tweenies™

Happy Birthday, Fizz!

BBC

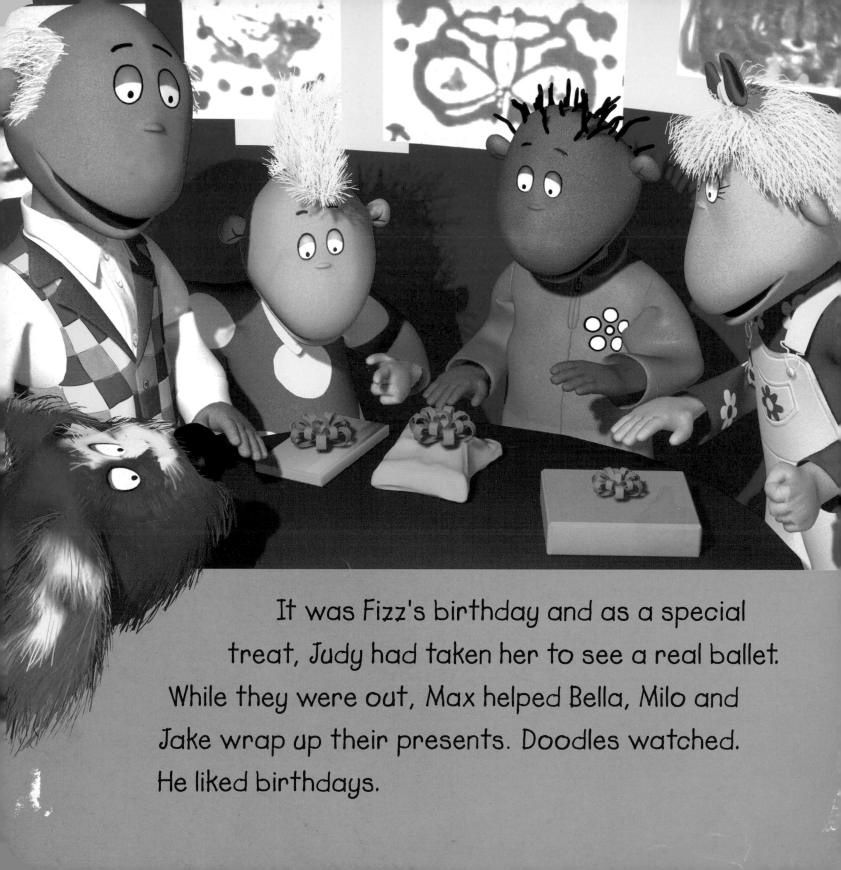

It was Fizz's birthday and as a special
treat, Judy had taken her to see a real ballet.
While they were out, Max helped Bella, Milo and
Jake wrap up their presents. Doodles watched.
He liked birthdays.

"Can I ever have a birthday present?" Jake asked Max.

"Of course you can," Max replied.

"Oh, good!" said Jake, and helped himself to the biggest one!

"No, Jake!" cried Bella.
"You can have a present
on YOUR birthday.
Today is Fizz's
birthday so SHE gets
the present!"

Max told the Tweenies that birthdays were extra-special days. Not only did you get presents but you were also another year older.

"Fizz is FOUR years old today," he told them.

The Tweenies helped Max get ready for the party. Milo found the party hats and hung up the streamers.

Bella blew up the balloons and
Jake helped Max set the table.

When everything was ready, they made Fizz a birthday card
with a big number four on the front.

"I've got a great idea," said Milo. "Why don't we stick four candles on Fizz's birthday cake?"

"Oh, yes!" cried Jake.

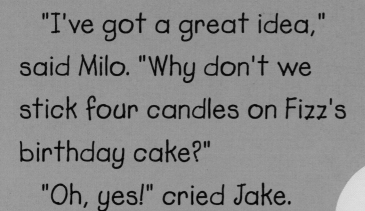

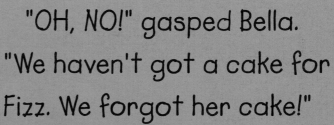

"OH, NO!" gasped Bella. "We haven't got a cake for Fizz. We forgot her cake!"

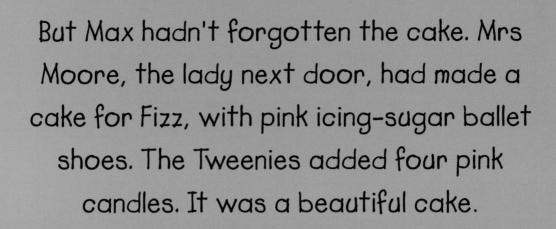

But Max hadn't forgotten the cake. Mrs Moore, the lady next door, had made a cake for Fizz, with pink icing-sugar ballet shoes. The Tweenies added four pink candles. It was a beautiful cake.

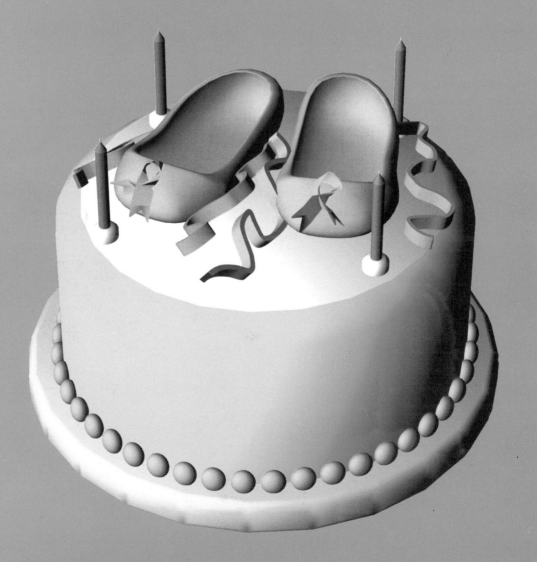

"What a shame it won't last," said Milo.

"Why won't it last?" asked Jake.

"Because we're going to EAT it, matie!" giggled Milo.

Max told the Tweenies that they couldn't eat the cake until Fizz had blown out the candles and made her birthday wish.

"Oh, I wish I could wish," sighed Jake.

"What would you wish for?" asked Max.

"Something really big and exciting," he replied.

"I know what I'd wish for," said Milo, and he made up a song about it . . .

"I wish I had a wish,
'cos then I'd wish
for a robot
to play in the park with me!"
he sang.

"I wish I had a wish,
'cos then I'd wish
for a star
to dance in the sky with me!
sang Bella.

"I wish I had a wish,
'cos then I'd wish
for a dragon
to come and live with me!"
sang Jake.

"I wish I had a wish,
'cos then I'd wish
for sausages
with chops and gravy for
my tea!"

sang Doodles.

When Fizz came back with Judy, she was thrilled to see her party decorations. "I can't wait to start my party!" she cried, and went to hang up her coat.

Then Fizz noticed the pink icing-sugar ballet shoes on the cake.
"What BEAUTIFUL ballet shoes! I wish..." she began.
But it was time to open the presents.

Bella gave her a jigsaw and
Milo gave her a box of
coloured crayons.

"Guess what my present is," said Jake.
The parcel felt soft and squishy. Inside was a big packet
of jelly babies.
"Thank you, Jake," Fizz said. "We can all share them."

Next, Fizz opened a present from Max and Judy. It was a song book and a tape.

"We can all sing along together," said Fizz.

When Judy lit the candles on the birthday cake, Max said he knew exactly which song they should sing.

"Happy birthday to you, happy birthday to you, happy birthday, dear Fizz, happy birthday to YOU!"

Fizz stared at her cake and made a secret wish. Then, with one big puff, she blew out ALL the candles!

At that very moment, Doodles raced in with a parcel and dropped it on the floor beside Fizz. "WOOF WOOF!" he barked. "Happy birthday, Fizz!"

"Thank you, Doodles!" said Fizz. She unwrapped the parcel and stared in amazement at Doodle's surprise gift.

"PINK BALLET SHOES!" she gasped.
"Doodles, you've made my birthday wish come true!"

THE END